W9-AVH-625

The Young Reader's Shakespeare

HAMLET

A Retelling by Adam McKeown

Illustrated by Sally Wern Comport

SCHOLASTIC INC.

New York Toronto London Auckland Sydney
Mexico City New Delhi Hong Kong Buenos Aires

BOOK DESIGN BY DEBORAH KERNER/DANCING BEARS DESIGN

No part of this publication may be reproduced in whole or in part, or stored in
a retrieval system, or transmitted in any form or by any means, electronic,
mechanical, photocopying, recording, or otherwise, without written
permission of the publisher. For information regarding permission, write to
Sterling Publishing Company, Inc., 387 Park Avenue South, New York, NY 10016.

ISBN 0-439-62654-4

Text copyright © 2003 by Adam McKeown.
Illustrations copyright © 2003 by Sally Wern Comport. All rights reserved.
Published by Scholastic Inc., 557 Broadway, New York, NY 10012, by
arrangement with Sterling Publishing Company, Inc. SCHOLASTIC and
associated logos are trademarks and/or registered trademarks of Scholastic Inc.

12 11 10 9 8 7 6 5 4   5 6 7 8 9/0

Printed in the U.S.A.   23

First Scholastic printing, January 2004

Contents

ABOUT SHAKESPEARE AND HAMLET

Little is known about the man most people consider the greatest writer in the history of the English language. We know that he was born in a small town near London called Stratford-upon-Avon sometime around April 23, 1564, and that he died in the same town on almost the same day in 1616. We know that he married when he was very young and had three children. We suspect he was educated, but we don't know where or for how long. He never enrolled in college but obviously studied English and Roman history and could probably read Latin quite well by today's standards. All we know is that sometime around 1589 he went to London to write plays and continued to do so, with a great deal of success, for the next twenty years.

Some people are not sure we know even that much. Shakespeare wrote an incredible number of plays and poems. He used more words than the average educated person many times over. He also invented words, hundreds of them —perhaps even more. It would be easy enough to believe that rather than one Shakespeare there were really four or five talented writers using the same name. In truth, Shakespeare did have help from some of his friends, and he borrowed most of the stories for his plays from other sources, but what he accomplished is no less staggering. Imagine writing a great book every six months twenty years in a row. That's about what Shakespeare did, and that's why we continue to read him four hundred years later.

The book you are about to read is based on his most famous play. One of these days—probably very soon—you will read it as Shakespeare wrote it or as it was performed in Shakespeare's lifetime. *Hamlet* is maybe the one work in all of English literature that everyone in the English-speaking world reads before graduating from secondary school. It was first performed around 1600, about halfway through Shakespeare's career, and it has been a favorite ever since.

This version of *Hamlet* is very much like the play. I have even left some of the more famous lines exactly as Shakespeare wrote them. One big difference between this version of *Hamlet* and the original is that Shakespeare wrote scripts for plays meant to be seen on stage while this book is a story meant to be read. Much of what you have to imagine while reading this book, Shakespeare's audiences would have seen with their own eyes. For this reason, I have had to say many of the things Shakespeare left unsaid.

Adding words to the most famous play written by the greatest writer of all time, however, is no easy task, especially since Shakespeare left us with almost no stage directions or other clues as to how his plays might have looked in performance. And sometimes the clues he does give make matters even more confusing. For instance, in *The Winter's Tale* Shakspeare gives the direction "Exit pursued by a bear." Scholars have been debating for centuries whether Shakespeare used a trained bear, an actor in a bear suit, or just some roaring sounds offstage. We just don't know.

To give you the most faithful rendition of *Hamlet* I could, I read many different editions, saw many different productions, and studied many books. But the real help came from other readers. Because I teach Shakespeare in college, I am fortunate to have been involved in hundreds of discussions about *Hamlet* with friends, students, and other teachers in the United States, Canada, and the U.K. In every discussion I learned a new way of thinking about *Hamlet*, and this book is a reflection of those discussions. I hope you will enjoy this book today because it is a good story, but what I really hope is that it will prepare you to read Shakespeare's *Hamlet* later on in your life and to answer the questions *Hamlet* raises about our world, our countries, our families, and ourselves.

Chapter One

"Who's there!?" Barnardo shouted.

"Reveal yourself first," returned a trembling voice through the fog.

Barnardo went forward, sliding one hand along the stone of the castle walls so he wouldn't lose his step in the gloom and fall.

"Don't come any farther!" said the voice.

"Francisco?"

"Is that you, Barnardo?"

"Yes, Francisco," Barnardo said. "It's midnight. I've come to relieve you."

The two groped forward in the darkness until their hands touched.

"Thanks, friend Barnardo," Francisco said. "It is so cold out here—and dark. And . . ." he looked around and lowered his voice, "terrifying."

In truth, Barnardo was a little frightened too, but he did not like to admit it, even to himself. "Why, have you seen something strange again?"

"Nothing, but . . ."

"Well, don't think anymore about it. Get to bed." Barnardo patted Francisco on the shoulder. "And if you see Horatio, let him know where I am."

Suddenly, footsteps scraped up the stairs behind Barnardo and Francisco. They drew their swords, crying, "Stop! Who goes there?"

"A friend," someone answered confidently. "And, like you, a loyal subject to the King of Denmark." The footsteps came closer. "Put away your swords."

"It's Horatio," said Barnardo, angry with himself for being so jumpy.

"I hope it's Horatio," said Francisco, still quaking.

Horatio was within inches of their noses before they could make out his face

through the fog. "Why so ill at ease, soldiers?" he asked, trying to hide his smile. "Have you seen this thing tonight?"

"So you don't believe us?" Francisco said.

"In a word, no," answered Horatio.

"The scholar is too smart to believe in ghosts," mocked Barnardo, nudging Francisco. "He thinks a couple of simple-minded soldiers just let their fears get the best of them."

"I never called you simple-minded," Horatio corrected. He may have been young and some said he was arrogant, but Horatio never judged anyone unfairly. "But I do think your senses were tricked by the fog and the darkness. It's the only logical explanation."

"See there," said Barnardo, "he thinks we were imagining things."

"No," said Francisco, lifting a trembling finger toward the far wall. His face was white and his eyes were wide. "See here! Do you call that imagination?"

"See what?" said Horatio turning. "Dear God!"

Above the castle wall, as if standing on the air itself, loomed the figure of an old warrior. He was dressed in full armor, and his white beard hung down almost to his waist. His hollow eyes burned like shiny black coals in his pale face. He seemed to stare at the petrified men, but he said nothing.

Francisco dropped down to his knees and prayed.

"Speak to it, Horatio," said Barnardo, "you're the one who knows all the big words."

Horatio swallowed the lump in his throat and stepped forward. "Who are you, spirit?" he demanded, trying to sound brave. "How dare you frighten these men? How dare you come in the shape of Denmark's dead king?"

The ghost vanished.

Barnardo and Francisco came up behind Horatio.

"Well, scholar," Barnardo said, "what do you think of our imaginations now?"

"If I didn't see it, I wouldn't have believed it," Horatio said, staring out at the empty darkness. "The presence of this specter in the shape of the old king means that something is very wrong in Denmark."

"We didn't need a ghost to tell us that," said Francisco. "The poor people of this kingdom have let their farms go to ruin preparing for war. Day and night we are busy building ships and guns. Even on Sundays we have to work. It's getting so we don't even recognize our own children when we come home."

"Yes," agreed Barnardo. "If the ghost is going to frighten us every night, at least he could tell us why we're working so hard. Or who we are even preparing to fight."

"I can tell you that," Horatio said. "Our old king, whose ghost we saw just now, captured all of Norway long ago—to satisfy his pride." Horatio shook his head. "Kings and their pride. Anyway, our old king and the King of Norway made a deal. The King of Norway would still rule over his kingdom, but when he died, the King of Denmark would inherit all the lands of Norway. But our old king passed away, as you know, and the King of Norway won't be far behind. Young Prince Fortinbras of Norway does not want to give his inheritance to the new king of Denmark, and so we are preparing to fight him. Or so the rumor goes."

"I guess the old king wants to keep fighting his old war," said Barnardo. "But if I had my way he and his old wars would stay dead and buried."

"You don't mean that, Barnardo," said Francisco, aghast.

"Peace, good soldiers. Look at the ghost not as a person but a sign," Horatio suggested. "The ancient authors agree that when something is wrong in the heart of a kingdom, all manner of supernatural phenomena occur. Why," he tried to remember a lecture he heard at the university, "in Rome, before Julius Caesar was murdered, shooting stars rained down from the heavens and the dead, still wrapped in their burial shrouds, crept out of their graves and . . ."

"Here it comes again!" cried Francisco.

As a great gust of wind roared over the battlements, the ghost appeared once more, peering at them with his empty black eyes.

"I'll strike at it!" yelled Barnardo, lifting his sword.

"Don't," cried Francisco, holding Barnardo back "It's the king!"

"It may not be the king," said Horatio, trying to be heard above the howling wind and the crash of the waves against the castle walls below. "Spirits can take many forms!"

"Then let me at it!" growled Barnardo.

"No," said Horatio, "let me speak to it. If it tries to get away, then strike it."

As if the ghost had heard what Horatio said, it turned and hurried away.

"It's running!" cried Francisco. "Like a guilty thief."

"I'll get it!" Barnardo said, pushing away Francisco and chasing after the specter into the darkness.

"Stop it if you can!" Horatio cried after Barnardo.

"I have him here," yelled Barnardo. "He's here!"

"No, he's still here," said Francisco, trying desperately to make sense of the whirl of bodies moving in the darkness.

"No," shouted Horatio, "he's over here! Back here!"

"No, here!" Barnardo roared.

"It's still here," whispered Francisco.

But the ghost was gone.

Chapter Two

Trumpets sounded and the doors of the great hall swung open to reveal Claudius, King of Denmark. Gertrude, his queen, held him by the right arm.

Tall and slender, Claudius bore himself with an elegant grace. His delicate lips smiled faintly beneath his thin moustache as he listened to the music play. He leaned over to Gertrude, kissed her soft cheek, and stepped into the hall.

Everybody rose.

"Please, ladies and gentlemen," Claudius called out, "Please remain seated. This is a time for joy and not for formality. What kind of king wants people to leap out of their chairs every time he walks into a room? Hmm?"

Gertrude gave the crowd a reassuring smile, and eventually the people began to talk in low, nervous whispers.

"Fill the glasses, boy," shouted Claudius. "It's time for a toast."

The little cupbearer did as he was told, filling everyone's class from a silver pitcher. Then Claudius lifted the goblet and spoke. "This is a sad and happy occasion. Sad in that Denmark has lost a great king, and I have lost a dear brother." He allowed a moment of silence for everyone to reflect on the old king. "But," Claudius went on brightly, "I assure you I am prepared to take up my brother's burden. If God allows, I will try to be for you and all of Denmark

a king not as great as he was, for that
would be impossible, but a good king,
a fair king, and a wise king."

The crowd cheered. The boy hurried
forward and refilled the king's cup.

"The queen, my brother's wife," Claudius
continued, "shall be the queen still." He
turned to Gertrude. "The ceremonies were
performed in the chapel yesterday. We are
married." He kissed Gertrude on the lips.

Gertrude stared out past the murmuring
crowd and let her eyes fall on the royal standard
of Denmark hanging from the far wall. She stood
proudly and raised her cup to her people.

And they cheered for her.

But there was one who did not cheer. In the corner,
by a table covered with meat pies and exotic fruits,
a young, dark-haired man stood silently watching.

"And now," Claudius went on, "we understand that
certain members of our court would ask some favors of our royal
person. These we will answer in time. First," he
said grandly, "the business of state calls. Osric!"

A dainty man with long, curly hair ran to the
king and doffed a velvet hat decorated with
feathers and gold spangles. "My liege," he said
bowing low.

"Go to the King of Norway and tell him that
we are aware that young Prince Fortinbras is
readying himself for war against Denmark. This
does not please our royal person. Remind Old
Norway of the agreement he made with my
brother. Go."

"I will obey, my liege!" said Osric, scurrying away.

"Now, then," Claudius stepped toward the throngs of lords and ladies in the great hall. "I understand Laertes has a request."

"Yes, my liege," said a neatly dressed, athletic young man with narrow-set eyes and a jaw that seemed too wide for his face. "Because I am first and foremost a loyal Dane, I came from France some weeks ago to pay my final respects to the old king. Since your royal highness's coronation followed soon after the funeral, I gladly remained longer than I had originally planned to honor the succession. News of your highness's intent to marry the queen kept me longer still, though I was glad to stay. But now my thoughts bend toward France, to which I will return, with your highness's permission."

"Well, what does your father say, Laertes? I may be a king, but I would never stand between a son and his father's wishes."

As Claudius put the question to young Laertes, an old man came forward, led by a beautiful young woman with a band of green silk around rivulets of golden hair. The old man put one hand on Laertes' shoulder as he came up beside him. "My lord, when a man's two pleasures in life are to satisfy every request of his son and to have his son forever by his side, what should a man do whose son has asked to leave?"

"Then one would take pleasure in so fine a daughter," remarked Claudius. "Good evening to you, pretty Ophelia."

Ophelia smiled silently and curtsied to the king.

Polonius looked around distractedly. "What was I saying? I know I was about to say something . . ."

Claudius rubbed his eyes. "You were saying something about sons and fathers, about what might a father do . . ."

"My lord . . ." interrupted Polonius, and then his voice trailed off.

Claudius sighed. Laertes rolled his eyes.

Gertrude stepped in, kindly. "You were asking should your son Laertes have your permission to go to France. Isn't that what you mean, dear old Polonius?"

"In short, my lady," Polonius answered, "yes, or I meant to say yes after I . . ."

"Excellent," roared Claudius. "Laertes, you have our consent and our best wishes. Leave whenever it pleases you."

"But before you go," Polonius interrupted, "let a father give a son some good advice."

Laertes huffed, eager to go back to his friends in France, but Ophelia came to his side and whispered, "Have patience, my brother."

"Now then, Laertes," said Polonius, after clearing his throat, "be sure to give every man your ear, but give few your voice. And beware of entering a quarrel, but once in, make your opponent beware of you. Do you understand me? Don't overdress."

As Polonius droned on, Claudius stared away. There was no point trying to interrupt him.

"Be friendly to everyone, but don't be everyone's friend. Now, listen." Polonius hesitated as if he had forgotten what he was about to say. "Oh, yes, neither a borrower nor a lender be. And, above all, to thine own self be true—because if you are true to yourself you cannot be false to anyone." He embraced his son. "Now go."

Laertes bowed to his father and the king and withdrew.

"Excellent," Claudius exclaimed, "and now . . ." He paused when his eyes met the eyes of the strange, silent young man at the other end of the hall.

"And now Hamlet," Claudius said. "Our nephew . . . and our son."

A hush fell and the crowd parted to allow the king an unobstructed view of the young man.

"You have asked to return to the university," Claudius said. "Our royal person would prefer your presence here in Denmark. You are to be king someday. It is crucial that you remain here and learn the duties of a king. Your desire to return to the university does not please your royal father and mother."

"My royal father is dead," said Hamlet coldly, letting his gaze fall on the floor.

Claudius moved toward Hamlet. "You won't find your father there on the ground, young Hamlet." He tried to remain cheery. "Come. Your father is here. Look on me as your father."

"I look on you as my father's brother and his wife's husband," said Hamlet. Claudius stiffened.

Gertrude came forward. "We are all sad for your father's loss. Why does it seem more difficult for you?"

"Seem, madam?" snapped Hamlet. "It doesn't seem difficult. It is."

"Look," said Claudius, losing patience but knowing he had to remain calm. "Your father lost his father. His father lost his father. Everyone loses a father. To mourn the death of a father becomes a son, but to remain melancholy and brooding, day after endless day, is unmanly!"

"Everyone will lose a father, Hamlet," Gertrude said gently.

"Yes, mother, but will everyone marry a dead father's brother?"

"Do not answer him, dearest queen," said Claudius, stepping between Gertrude and Hamlet.

The queen pushed away Claudius. "I am married to your father's brother, and so I am still married to the king. You are my son"—she smiled—"and so the king is still your father." She looked up again at the royal standard hanging over Hamlet's head, and then she stared deeply into her son's eyes. "My son, the Prince of Denmark. Won't you stay here, just for a little while longer?"

Hamlet turned his face from Gertrude's. "Of course I will always obey you, Mother."

"Good enough," said Claudius, though he wondered if Hamlet was being sincere. "Hamlet, you have made us very happy. Now, everyone," he shouted, "be merry!"

Chapter Three

Hamlet remained alone as the party went on. He couldn't eat or drink. Every piece of food he put into his mouth tasted like paste, everything he drank tasted like poison. He wanted so much for the party to end, but the king had ordered everyone to be merry, and so the party went on. Eventually he went to the window and looked out upon the sea. How could he marry a brother's wife, he thought? How could she marry a husband's brother? And so soon? A month, a little month, after his father died! Was this the way the world worked? he wondered, vowing never to be part of it. He watched the surf raging below and imagined himself falling.

"Good evening, my lord," came a voice behind him.

Hamlet turned. "Horatio! That's friend and not lord to you, friend." He threw his arms around Horatio. "What tore you away from the university and brought you to this horrible place?"

"Your father's funeral, my lord."

"You mock me, Horatio. You came to see my mother's wedding."

"The one did follow quickly upon the other."

Hamlet frowned and turned slowly back toward the window.

"I . . . I should not have mentioned your father," Horatio said. "Forgive me."

"You do not need to be sorry, friend." Hamlet sighed. "I see him everywhere, even without you recalling him to my mind. I see him right now."

Horatio rushed to the window. "Where do you see him?"

Hamlet looked with confusion at his friend. "I meant I imagine I see him—

as he was before he died. I cannot get him out of my mind. That's what I meant."

"Oh."

Hamlet was puzzled at Horatio's reaction. "What did you mean?"

"Nothing, my lord."

"Tell me," insisted Hamlet.

Horatio looked around to make sure no one was watching them and then led Hamlet to the back of the hall and down a stairway. There Horatio told his friend about the ghost he had seen the night before.

"And you say he wore armor?" Hamlet asked, astonished.

"Fully armed," answered Horatio.

"And you are sure it was my father?"

"I am sure it was an apparition that looked like your father," Horatio explained. "What it was I could not determine. It fled when I tried to speak to it."

"Perhaps it will speak to me," said Hamlet.

"My lord—my friend," said Horatio, "we cannot know whether the specter is your father's spirit or a demon taking his form. In your state of distress" —Horatio chose his words carefully—"you might be too ready to believe it is your father."

"I have a little sense left, Horatio," said Hamlet. "I want you to bring me to the place tonight. If it is my father's ghost, he may have some important message. And if it is a spirit taking his form, it could mean that something is wrong here in Denmark. Either way, I will speak to it."

"My lord, I—"

"Your friend," corrected Hamlet. "And as my friend I want you to help me. Come to my chamber before midnight."

"I will wake you."

"I won't be asleep."

Chapter Four

The wind howled in the gloom of a starless night as Horatio and Hamlet crept out onto the parapet. Five hundred feet below the sea frothed and broke against the rock on which the castle had been built long ago. The cold bit through their heavy cloaks and seemed to chill the marrow in their bones.

"Where is the watchman?" asked Hamlet.

"Ahead," answered Horatio.

"Who goes there?" cried a frightened voice. It was Francisco.

"Friends," said Horatio, moving forward through the mist.

"Good Horatio, and . . ." Francisco caught sight of the young prince and quickly swept his cap off his head as he dropped to a knee, "your lordship."

"Stand, good fellow," Hamlet said, helping Francisco back to his feet. "You can't keep watch from down there."

"Have you seen anything tonight?" asked Horatio.

"No, thank God," Francisco said.

"What time is it?" wondered Hamlet.

"Almost midnight," answered Horatio.

"Well, if it will make an appearance tonight it will be soon or not at all."

As Hamlet peered into the darkness above the battlements, a glimmering shape seemed to step forward from behind the black

curtain of night. It moved toward him. It was his father, armed from head to foot and carrying his bloody sword.

"Angels and ministers of grace defend us!" Hamlet gasped.

Francisco cowered in terror.

The ghost pointed at Hamlet and waved him forward.

"It beckons me," said Hamlet.

"Don't go," replied Horatio.

"D-d-d-don't follow it, my lord," stuttered Francisco.

The cold, black eyes of the ghost bore into Hamlet's soul.

"I'll go," Hamlet said.

"Think, Hamlet," Horatio said, taking his friend by the shoulders. "This could be a devil in your father's form! Look, it calls you toward the highest battlement. What if there it assumes some horrible shape and, in the darkness and confusion, you tumble over the side?"

"I'm going!" said Hamlet, pushing away Horatio.

"No, my lord, you will not!" Francisco shouted, knowing it was not his place to give orders to the prince but not knowing what else to do.

Horatio wrapped his arms around Hamlet from behind. Francisco moved in to help him.

"Unhand me, gentlemen!" Hamlet drew his sword. "I'll make a ghost of any man who tries to stop me."

Horatio and Francisco stepped back.

"My soul is immortal," Hamlet said in a low voice, "so it cannot be harmed by devils or ghosts or the wind or the waves. And as for my life . . ." He met the eyes of the ghost and then looked at the men in front of him. "It isn't worth much to me right now."

He sheathed his sword and walked slowly toward the glimmering specter.

As Hamlet followed the apparition deeper and deeper into the darkness, Horatio's words kept coming back to him. What if this is a devil in the shape of my father? But why should I be afraid if I truly believe that my soul is immortal and that my own life is not worth very much? Easier to say a thing like that surrounded by the safety of friends, Hamlet thought, than out here on the lonely battlements with only the roar of the wind and water as companions. He shivered and made a decision.

"I'll go no further!" he declared.

"Listen." The rumbling voice of the phantom echoed against the stone of the battlements and seemed to Hamlet as if it was coming from the walls of the castle itself.

"I will," said Hamlet meekly.

"Soon I must return to the burning flames," said the ghost.

"The flames! Oh, poor ghost!" Hamlet thought about his father writhing in pain in the purgatorial fires.

"Don't pity me," roared the ghost. "Avenge me!"

"Avenge?"

"Avenge, Hamlet. Avenge your father's murder!"

"Murder?" Hamlet felt himself grow faint. "My father. Murdered."

An unearthly green light shot through the ghost, and his face twisted with rage. "Murdered, Hamlet, murdered before I had a chance to say my prayers, to repent my sins, to make peace with the Almighty!" His hollow eyes fixed themselves on Hamlet. "Murder most foul! Murdered by that scheming beast, my brother!"

"Oh, my prophetic soul!" Hamlet had not allowed himself to believe it, but in his heart he suspected it. "Was it . . . my uncle?"

"Poisoned," moaned the ghost, "poisoned by my brother while I slept in the garden. And now he wears my crown and calls my queen his wife, while I return each dawn to the purifying flames until my sins are burned away!"

"Oh, father," cried Hamlet, "what shall I do?"

"Revenge, Hamlet," roared the ghost, lifting his sword high, "seek revenge for my murder. Pay back my brother for his crime."

From within the castle, far below, the cry of a rooster pierced the night. Hamlet looked out upon the sea where, on the horizon, the sky began to glow pink.

"My hour has come," said the ghost. "Farewell, Hamlet, remember me."

The spirit vanished.

Hamlet dropped to the ground.

Horatio and Francisco came running up toward him.

"My lord, we were worried," said Francisco.

"We have been looking for you for hours," added Horatio. "Where have you been for so long?"

"For so long?" wondered Hamlet. Had so much time gone by? Hamlet lifted himself to his feet and stared at the spot where the ghost had stood.

"What did the spirit say?" asked Horatio.

"Terrible things," Hamlet replied.

"What is it, my lord?" begged Francisco.

Hamlet unsheathed his sword. "Swear on my blade that you will tell no one what you have seen tonight."

"We swear, my lord. We swear," said Horatio and Francisco.

"On my blade, friends," insisted Hamlet, "put your swords on mine and swear."

"Swear!" the voice came from the stones. It was the ghost. His father.

Hamlet went pale.

"What is it, Hamlet?" asked Horatio.

"The prince is not well," said Francisco. "Let's get him inside."

"It is nothing, good soldier," said Hamlet. "But leave us. You have done your duty here."

Francisco bowed and did as he was told.

"Swear!" came the voice again.

"Do you not hear the old fellow thundering?"

"Nothing, my lord, I hear nothing."

Was he hearing things? Hamlet wondered. If so, had he seen things too? He wasn't sure any more. "Horatio, you did see a shape like my father tonight, didn't you?"

"Yes," answered Horatio, "a shape like your father in every detail."

"And if I tell you what he said, you'll swear never to repeat it?"

"Yes, my lord."

"Swear!" Hamlet could feel the stones of the castle shake.

"And you still hear nothing?"

"Only the wind and the waves—and you, my lord."

"Your friend," said Hamlet. "Now, swear."

"I swear!" cried Horatio.

"Good," said Hamlet. "Now listen. If the ghost was honest, I have bloody work to do. But first I have to put the ghost's words to the test. I will pretend to have lost my mind—if everyone believes I am mad, I can say whatever I want to my uncle. Maybe I can provoke him into admitting or trick him into revealing that he murdered the king, my father."

"Your uncle?" Horatio said, startled by his friend's words. "Murdered his own brother? I don't believe it."

"You didn't believe in ghosts either," Hamlet said. "But there are more things in heaven and earth, Horatio, than are dreamt of in your philosophy. I tell you, something is rotten in the state of Denmark."

In low whispers Hamlet related to Horatio everything the ghost had told him.

Chapter Five

Polonius concealed himself behind a bush and watched Hamlet wander through the garden holding a book and talking to himself.

"To be, or not to be," Hamlet asked out loud. "Is it nobler to bear the end-less agony of life or to end one's life, to die, to sleep?" He was putting on a show of madness for the benefit of Polonius, who was always somewhere watching, and yet the words struck him deeply. Even though Horatio had his doubts, Hamlet believed that the ghost had told him the truth, that Claudius had murdered his father—which meant that he was bound by honor to kill Claudius in return. Yet he did not think he had the courage to do it. And, then again, what if he was wrong? What if the ghost were a devil trying to trick him into killing the king? The king, his uncle and his mother's husband? How was he supposed to know? To kill a king was the worst crime a man could commit in the eyes of the state, and to kill a relative was the worst crime a man could commit in the eyes of God. How could he do it based on the word of a ghost?

The questions were overwhelming. It would have been much easier, Hamlet thought, if he had fallen over the battlements into the sea. That way he wouldn't have to worry about the decisions he had to make—or anything else. And perhaps death would be like a sound sleep after a hard day. Perhaps in the sleep of death one could even dream. But death was not sleep. His father was dead, and instead of sleeping he walked the cold battlements all night and returned each morning to the fires.

But maybe that was a lie, too. Maybe the ghost was a devil trying to play on his sympathies. Maybe he was supposed to imagine that by murdering his uncle he could save his father! Devils did things like that. And who knew what

tortures were in store for someone who killed a king, a king who was also his own uncle? But if the ghost was lying, did those tortures exist at all? Was there anything after death? Was there anyone who could say? No. Death was an undiscovered country from which no traveler had ever returned.

"Father," Ophelia cried, running up behind Polonius.

"Be quiet!" Polonius hissed, capping the young woman's mouth with his hand.

Hamlet looked around pretending not to notice the commotion.

"Although this seems like madness there is a method in it," Polonius mumbled. Slowly he removed his palm from his daughter's face. "What do you want?" he demanded.

"Father," Ophelia whispered, "I was sewing in my room when Hamlet came to me, his shirt unbuttoned and his hair a mess. He . . . he held me by the wrists and stared without saying anything."

"That must be why he is here walking alone in this distracted manner," Polonius said to himself. "And did you return his love letters like I told you?"

"I did, father," Ophelia replied. "I gave him back the whole box."

"Good," said Polonius.

As Ophelia watched Hamlet press the book against his heart again, tears welled up in her eyes. "Oh, father," she said, "I am afraid I have upset him."

Her father noticed the change in her voice. "Don't weep over him. He's a prince. You're a foolish, ordinary girl. He may say he loves you, but he'll never marry you. He can't." His eyes were still focused on Hamlet. "But I do think you have driven him into this madness."

The tears were now rolling down Ophelia's cheeks. "He said he loved me."

"Quiet!" said Polonius. "If you believed him, then you are a fool. Worse, you have made a fool of me for raising such a foolish daughter."

"Oh, father," Ophelia murmured. "You don't think he really loves me?"

"Go to the king. Tell him that Hamlet has lost his mind because he is in love with you and you returned his letters. Get! And don't dawdle!"

Ophelia did as she was told. She tiptoed out of the garden, but her father's words rang in her ears. Hamlet does love me, she thought. I know he does. She reached for a little purse fastened to her sash in which she kept her favorite letter from Hamlet, but once she opened it she remembered that she had returned that letter too. Staring into the empty purse she began to weep uncontrollably. She ran all the way to the king, hoping the wind would dry her tears before she got there.

Claudius sat on his throne, Gertrude beside him. Before him stood two men about Hamlet's age. They were handsome, swashbuckling fellows. Each wore a moustache waxed into curls at the tips, but they were too young to grow beards. Bright new swords hung from their shiny black belts.

"I called you here because you two are Hamlet's friends," the king began. "He trusts you. And so I hope you might be able to learn more about his sudden madness."

"We will learn what we can, my liege," said one.

"We will obey you, dread sovereign," said the other.

"Thanks, Rosencrantz," the king said, holding his hand out to the first man.

"That's Guildenstern," whispered Gertrude. "The other one is Rosencrantz."

"Of course," the king apologized. "Thanks, Guildenstern and gentle Rosencrantz."

The two men bowed low and left the hall just as Polonius rushed in with Ophelia.

"My liege," Polonius exclaimed, "I have discovered the cause of Hamlet's insanity."

Gertrude ran to meet Polonius, eager to hear what he had learned, but

when she saw Ophelia looking so distraught, her heart filled with pity. "What is it, dear girl?" she asked, putting an arm around Ophelia.

"What it is, my lady," Polonius said, "is the matter about which I have come, the matter about which I sent my daughter to you, and the matter because of which she collapsed outside your hall on her way here. It is the matter of Prince Hamlet's madness. No less a matter."

"Well, what is it?" snapped Claudius. He was in no mood for Polonius's babbling.

"What is what, my liege?" asked Polonius.

"The matter!" the king roared.

"Why, the matter over which Hamlet is mad," said Polonius.

"What is the matter, Polonius? The matter!" The king stood. "Out with it!"

"What is wrong with my son?" Gertrude asked gently.

"Why, that's what I've come to tell you, my lady," said Polonius.

"Oh, for heaven's sake!" cried Claudius, sitting heavily back down onto his throne.

"I know, old Polonius," Gertrude said, "and we are ready to listen."

"Of course," Polonius said. "In short, Hamlet is in love. In love with my daughter here. Now," he raised his finger, "I know what you are thinking. There is no way a prince would fall in love with an ordinary girl—and, believe me, I told her many times that she isn't good enough for Hamlet—but he has fallen in love with her anyway. I told her to return his love letters, and when she did so, he lost his mind."

Ophelia, who had been listening in silence, started to cry again.

"Do you agree with this?" the king asked her.

"I agree with my father, always," she said, trying to hold back her tears.

Gertrude held Ophelia tightly. "Hamlet is in love with her," she said, "I can see it in his eyes."

Ophelia sank into the queen's arms. "I know I am an ordinary girl," she whispered, "but I thought he loved me."

"Hush, sweet Ophelia," the queen said, "you are not an ordinary girl."

"But do you think it is love that is driving Hamlet mad?" asked the king.

"There is only one way to know," Polonius answered. "We will test my theory. You have seen how Hamlet walks about talking to himself? I say we send my daughter to him when he is in one of his fits. We'll make her say something that will upset him further—something like, 'stop crying out my name' or 'I never loved you' or 'I love another man more than I love you' or 'your letters were poorly written' or . . ."

"We get the idea," interrupted the king, seeing how her father's words hurt Ophelia. "We'll save that strategy for another time. Your daughter is in no condition to assail Hamlet."

"Then, my liege, we will have Ophelia start a quarrel with him and . . ."

"We will ask her to talk with him. That should be sufficient. But we'll do it later." The king rose from his seat. "Perhaps Rosenstern and Guildencrantz have had more luck with Hamlet."

The queen raised an eyebrow

"Rosencrantz and Guildenstern?" asked Claudius.

The queen nodded.

"Of course. Perhaps Rosencrantz and Guildenstern can tell us more about Hamlet. Come," he said. "Let's find them."

As they were leaving, Ophelia spoke to the queen in a voice so soft no one else could hear, "Why must I trick the lord Hamlet, my lady?"

"Because he is the Prince of Denmark," Gertrude whispered back, "and Denmark cannot have a mad prince. You must do it. Remember that if love is strong enough to make Hamlet mad it will be strong enough to make him well again. Have patience. All will be well if you and I perform our duty to Denmark." She kissed Ophelia's forehead and led her out toward the garden.

31

Chapter Six

"What are you reading?" Rosencrantz called out to Hamlet as he came down the stairs leading to the garden. "It must be a good book."

"Words," Hamlet answered without looking to see who was talking to him. "Words, words, words."

"And what do they say?" asked Guildenstern, who found a flat rock and skipped it in the lily pond. "I myself never cared much for reading words."

"I am not reading them," Hamlet replied in a dreamy voice. "I am listening to them."

"They are talking to you, then?" Rosencrantz said, unsheathing his sword and lopping off the head of a daisy. "Talking words. Have you ever heard of that, Guildenstern?"

"Never in my life, Rosencrantz."

"Guildenstern?" Hamlet said. "And Rosencrantz." He whirled about and saw his old friends. "Rosencrantz and Guildenstern!" He went to them. "How good it is to see you. What brings you here to the castle?"

"To see you, my lord," said Guildenstern.

"To see me?" There was something in Guildenstern's voice that made Hamlet think there was more to the story. "To see me and for no other reason?"

"No other reason," confirmed Rosencrantz.

"Come," said Hamlet, "the king didn't send for you? He didn't ask you to go out and talk with his nephew-son who has lately lost his mind?"

Rosencrantz looked at Guildenstern.

"I guess I have my answer," said Hamlet.

"My lord," said Rosencrantz, embarrassed at having been caught in a lie, "the king did ask us to come here and talk to you."

"But only because he is concerned about you," added Guildenstern.

"As is your mother, the queen," said Rosencrantz.

"Oh, well then," exclaimed Hamlet. "If a man may lie because of what concerns the king, then might not a man kill for what concerns a king's brother?" He burst out laughing before Ronsencrantz or Guildenstern had time to answer. He wanted them to think he was mad, too. He could see that they were no longer his friends. They had not come to help him but to manipulate him. He could stand being spied on by Polonius, but not being deceived by people who were supposed to be his old friends. "But listen, since you two were so good to come all this way just to see me, I'll tell you a secret." He leaned in. "My uncle-father and aunt-mother are deceived."

"How deceived?" asked Guildenstern.

"I am mad only when the wind blows north. When the wind blows south I can tell east from west."

"So you aren't really mad, my lord?" asked Rosencrantz. You could have fooled me! he thought.

"No, no," Hamlet said lightly, climbing a tree and hanging by his knees from a branch. "The world looks exactly as it should. Upside down. Doesn't it look right to you?"

"My lord," Guildenstern ventured, remembering the task the king had assigned him, "we must know the cause of your madness."

"The king," said Hamlet. "Just as he is the cause of your curiosity."

"My lord," began Rosencrantz.

"The players have arrived!" came a loud voice from the castle gate.

"The players?" asked Hamlet.

"We should have mentioned it, my lord, knowing how much you love plays," explained Guildenstern.

"The tragedians of the city," Rosencrantz went on. "We ran across them on their way here and asked them to come and put on a play for you."

"He who plays the king shall be welcome!" cried Hamlet, letting go of the branch and landing on his feet. "Send them to my chamber. I have written a play I want them to enact, and there is so little time to rehearse."

"You've written a play, my lord?" asked Rosencrantz.

"Yes, I wrote it upon the air while I was walking in the garden getting some fresh paper," he held his book to his face upside down and pretended to read. "It's about a king's nephew who goes mad . . . well, I don't want to spoil the ending for you." He slammed the book shut. "Send the players to the prince's chamber. I am sure he will join them if he doesn't lose his mind on the way there."

Hamlet strutted away.

Rosencrantz and Guildenstern shook their heads and followed him out of the garden.

Chapter Seven

"And you could gather nothing from him? Nothing at all that might explain this madness," the king asked. "Nothing?"

"Well . . ." Rosencrantz shifted uneasily on his feet.

"Speak, if you have something to say!" ordered Claudius.

"My liege," Guildenstern answered cautiously. "He did say that 'the king' was the cause of his madness. Whether he meant your majesty or his late departed father I could not tell."

"It is as I feared," said Gertrude, standing by the throne. "The cause is none other than his father's death and our hasty marriage."

The king took a deep breath. He suspected the same. "Thank you, gentlemen. Please leave us."

Rosencrantz and Guildenstern bowed and left.

"What do you think, Polonius?" asked the king, hoping there was another answer.

"Love, I say," Polonius replied, coming forward. "I still say it is his love for my daughter that has driven him mad. Fortunately, we have been granted an opportunity to prove as much. Hamlet has penned yet another private letter to my daughter, professing his love." Polonius seemed delighted by his own deviousness. "I was watching through the keyhole of her bedchamber, and there I saw her take the letter from her purse. I have ordered her to return the letter to the prince. She is sitting in the hallway outside this very room, waiting for Hamlet to come to her. Let us all listen at the door and determine for ourselves whether or not love is at the root of the prince's madness."

They all followed Polonius to the door and waited.

Hamlet did not notice Ophelia as he strode up the hall with several of the players in train. "Recite your lines exactly as I have written them," he said, "without improvisation. And I want clear pronunciation, with good tone—I don't want to hear anyone shouting like a town crier. And no overacting either, do you understand? Too many actors saw the air with their hands and work themselves into a passion for an audience which is usually asleep anyway or waiting for song and dance. Avoid it."

"We have some experience putting on plays, my lord," said an old actor, the leader of the troop. "Don't worry about us."

"My lord Hamlet," said Ophelia meekly.

"Ophelia?" Hamlet was surprised to see her there. "I will meet you in the great hall, fellows," said Hamlet to the actors, "go and rehearse your parts and remember what I told you."

"Aye, my lord," the old actor replied, bowing.

They left Hamlet alone with Ophelia.

"My lord," she said, "I am returning the letter you sent me. It . . ." She could barely say the words. "It does not please me." She held the letter out to Hamlet.

He looked at the paper in her delicate hand. "I gave you no letter."

"You did, my lord. You gave it to me this morning. And I am returning it to you." Her hand began to tremble. "Please take it."

"You have mistaken Hamlet for your father, Ophelia," Hamlet said. "I gave a letter to a woman who loved me. You love only your father, so it follows that the letter is not mine."

Ophelia could not stand it any longer. She wanted to keep the letter, to kiss it, to press it against her heart. She wanted to tell Hamlet that she loved him more than anything, and that she was only doing as she was told. But then, she thought, her father would be furious.

Hamlet watched the paper flutter to the floor. "I once said I loved you," he said.

"And you once made me believe you did," answered Ophelia.

"Well," said Hamlet, "I lied. Just like you lied."

Ophelia felt the tears coming. Wouldn't someone step forward and put an end to this cruel charade? she wondered. Anyone?

"You are faithless! You promise your love to one man knowing full well that you are bound to another!" Hamlet stooped and stared into Ophelia's swollen eyes. "And where is that other man now, your father?"

"At home," Ophelia said.

"Go to him!" Hamlet yelled. "Marry him while you're there. Why not, if you love him so much? Besides, in this castle a man may marry his brother's wife, so why might you not marry your father? Why, you might marry my uncle too. If you love only where your obedience lies, then you and all of Denmark might as well marry the king. My mother did." He was speaking without thinking. Where before he had been pretending to be insane, now he really knew what it felt like to be insane, to lose control, to have words fly out of his heart before his brain had a chance to temper them. "She married my father, too, when he was the king, but now that he is dead, well, there will always be a new king to replace the old one when he dies. My uncle made sure of that!"

"Oh, my sweet lord Hamlet!" cried Ophelia.

"Your sweet lord Polonius is at home!" Hamlet kicked the letter and stormed away.

"Love?!" bellowed Claudius as he, Gertrude, and Polonius rushed forward

from behind the door. "He's not in love! Anyone can see that!" Claudius shivered. Had Hamlet discovered his crime? "Call the guards," he said. "I want Hamlet followed—for his own safety. In this mood he could destroy himself or someone else. Go!"

"I still say he is in love, my lord," insisted Polonius.

"And I said go," growled Claudius.

Polonius rushed out.

Claudius stomped away, wondering if Hamlet had figured out what he had done, and if so, what to do with Hamlet now.

Chapter Eight

"If you wanted the whole castle to believe you are completely out of your wits, then you have succeeded," Horatio said to Hamlet as the two watched the final dress rehearsal of the play.

"Let them believe it," said Hamlet. "Eavesdropping fools. I let the guards find me sleeping on the parapet, and when they nudged me awake I acted as if I were newborn. I told them I fell asleep there when the sun came up and remembered nothing before that? Everyone believes a madman, or at least they believe he believes himself, and so they do not question him. And soon they will be here to watch the play I have written, not wanting to risk upsetting me by refusing. But they'll wish they had refused once they see it."

"Why, my lord?"

"Because, Horatio, the play is something like the murder of my father. It is the story of Lucianus, nephew to King Gonzago. Lucianus poisons the king while he sleeps in the garden and then marries Gonzago's queen."

"Hamlet, this will upset them all."

"That's the point." Hamlet looked around to make sure they would not be overheard. "I want you to watch my uncle as the play unfolds. If he grows pale or reacts to the murder scene, then we will know that the ghost we saw is an honest ghost." Hamlet's voice became raspy and deep. "And then I know what I have to do."

"Murder, Hamlet? Don't even think it!" exclaimed Horatio.

"It's all I can think of," Hamlet said.

Trumpets sounded and the doors of the hall opened. Claudius and Gertrude walked in, followed by Polonius, Ophelia, Rosencrantz, Guildenstern, and other lords and ladies.

"And now the play begins," Hamlet said. "Watch him, Horatio. Watch him closely."

Hamlet messed up his hair, loosened his stockings so that they hung down around his ankles, and stumbled forth to meet the audience. "No, no, no, no, no," he scolded, "don't come in until the director gives you the cue! Didn't we rehearse? Only you, fair lady, got your part right." He planted a kiss on Ophelia's lips. "A faithful lover . . ."

"See that, my liege," Polonius whispered to Claudius, "he's still obsessed with my daughter."

"Hamlet," Claudius said, ignoring Polonius, "the stage is behind you. We are the audience, not the actors."

"Oh, pardon," Hamlet bowed theatrically, "a foolish mistake and one I should have recognized immediately. You wouldn't make a very convincing king, would you?"

Claudius bristled.

"He's mad, husband," assured Gertrude. "Let him be."

The queen led Claudius to his seat, and when everyone else had settled in the play began.

Hamlet watched the actors play the parts he had written for them, half hoping that the king would have no reaction to them. If the ghost lied, thought Hamlet, then he would not have to kill his uncle . . . But what then? His mother still married his father's brother within a month after his death. Ophelia still rejected his love. His friends could no longer be trusted. Even if the ghost lied, his life would still be miserable.

Just then the play arrived at the murder scene. The actor playing Lucianus crept silently into the make-believe garden where the actor playing the king pretended to sleep. He lifted a phial of poison and poured it into the sleeping king's ear.

"Stop the play!" shouted Claudius, leaping to his feet.

"Hamlet, you are mad! Come away, Gertrude!" He grabbed the queen hard by the arm and led her out of the hall. "Give me some light!"

Polonius and Rosencrantz hurried after the king with torches, and the actors, fearing some punishment, made for the exits, too. Guildenstern tried to hold them back, but was shoved into a stand of torches that had been illuminating the stage, knocking them to the ground as he fell. Guildenstern quickly stifled the flames with his coat, but with the hall cast into darkness, everyone was running into everyone else. Shouts rose. Confusion reigned.

When at last the hall had emptied, Hamlet looked up from a pile of broken chairs. In the flickering light he saw Horatio.

"It would seem the ghost was honest, my lord," Horatio said.

"And so let us hope I am brave," replied Hamlet.

Chapter Nine

"I like it not!" Claudius paced back and forth in front of Rosencrantz and Guildenstern. "It is not safe to let his madness range any further. You heard how his thoughts have grown violent. A nephew killing a king?! The play might as well have been a death threat. Therefore"—he withdrew a sealed warrant from his pocket—"I have arranged for him to go to England." He handed the warrant to Rosencrantz. "You two will accompany him. Give this paper to the English king upon your arrival. Now, go prepare yourselves."

"We will, my liege." Rosencrantz and Guildenstern bowed and stepped away.

Polonius came into the throne room as the two young men were leaving. "My lord," called Polonius, "the queen is greatly upset."

"Everyone is greatly upset, Polonius!"

"But I believe we can use the queen's distress to learn more about Hamlet's madness."

"I know all I care to know about Hamlet's madness," said Claudius. "I am sending him to England. There he will either recover his wits or at least pose no threat to our royal person." It had crossed Claudius's mind to arrest and execute Hamlet, but if he did he knew he would lose the loyalty of Gertrude, and without the loyalty of the queen whom all the people loved he would lose the loyalty of Denmark.

"I have spoken with the queen," Polonius went on as if the king had said nothing. "I will hide behind an arras in her bedchamber. Rosencrantz and Guildenstern will fetch him, and when he arrives I will secretly note what

passes between him and the queen. Though I am sure it all goes back to my daughter."

Claudius eyed Polonius with disgust and pity. Clearly, the old man liked spying for its own sake. Why could not Gertrude be trusted to relate what passed between herself and her son? It was as if Polonius lived for hiding behind bushes and doors and curtains to see what other people were doing. But Claudius was too disturbed to argue the point. He just wanted Polonius to leave him alone.

"Do as you think best," he said, turning away before Polonius had time to say anything more.

"My lord!" hollered Guildenstern as he and Rosencrantz approached Hamlet in the walkway outside the great hall.

"Musicians!" said Hamlet, as if he were delirious.

"No, my lord," snapped Rosencrantz. He was getting tired of Hamlet's antics. "We are your friends, not musicians. We have come to escort you to your mother's bedchamber, and then you must prepare to go to England."

"Not musicians, indeed," returned Hamlet, "you must be kings if you think you can order around a prince." He grinned.

Guildenstern sighed in frustration. "We are not kings, my lord."

"Then you are musicians," said Hamlet. "I knew it."

"Will you come with us, my lord? You will like England." Rosencrantz stepped up to Hamlet and smiled pleasantly. "We used to be friends. Won't you trust us to take you to England?"

Guildenstern came up beside Rosencrantz. "If we seem upset with you it is only because we care. Won't you come with us? Won't you, old friend?"

"Tell me, friend musician," said Hamlet thrusting a recorder into Guildenstern's hands, "can you play some notes for me on this instrument?"

"My lord, I cannot," said Guildenstern.

"I pray you," insisted Hamlet.

"Believe me, I cannot."

"I do beseech you."

"I know no touch of it, my lord." Guildenstern was getting annoyed again.

"It is as easy as lying," said Hamlet. "Press the vents with your fingers and thumbs, give it breath with your mouth, and it will discourse most eloquent music. Look, don't you see the stops?"

"But I have not the skill, my lord."

"Why, look you now," Hamlet growled, tearing the recorder out of Guildenstern's hands. "How unworthy a thing you make of me. You would play upon me, you would seem to know my stops, you would pluck out the heart of my mystery, you would sound me from the lowest to the highest note! There is much excellent music in this little instrument," he shook the recorder in Guildenstern's face, "and yet you cannot make it speak. God's blood, do you think I am easier to play upon than a pipe?"

He threw the instrument down, and it shattered at Guildenstern's feet.

Chapter Ten

As Hamlet stepped through the castle atrium on his way to his mother's bed-chamber, he began to wonder again if he really was going mad. His conversation with Rosencrantz and Guildenstern might have sounded like madness to someone else, and yet to him it made perfect sense. And for that matter, the idea of killing a king might seem like madness to anyone, but, under the circumstances, it too made perfect sense. Maybe he was the one sane person in a mad world. Maybe all madmen thought that of themselves. No, he concluded, the world was mad. His uncle had killed his father and married his mother. Ophelia, Rosencrantz, and Guildenstern—people he had trusted as his friends—were all, each in his or her own way, agents for the corrupt and murderous king. No less so than Polonius was. No, he was not mad, he decided—he was all too sane. "The time is out of joint," he said aloud as he mounted the stairs toward the sleeping chambers, "and cursed spite that ever I was born to set it right."

Hamlet made straight for his mother's bedchamber at the far end of the hall, but he had to pass his uncle's and his own on the way. He expected to find the door to his uncle's room closed, since Claudius now slept in the room that had been his father's, but the door stood partially open. Within Hamlet saw the man himself, kneeling with his back to the door.

Hamlet reached into his jacket and pulled out a dagger. Now might I do it, he thought, and crept toward the king.

"Oh, my offense is rank," the king whispered, his hands folded together in prayer. "A brother's murder! Is there no way I can be forgiven? Why, God, why did You make a creature like a man? Why make us smart enough to know right

from wrong and not strong enough to do right? You should have made us as stupid as the animals or as strong as Yourself! Why leave us stuck in between?"

Hamlet moved closer.

"What kind of prayer can I make?" Claudius's voice began to rise. "Shall I ask You to forgive me for murdering my brother? That cannot work since I still have his crown and his queen—and these I could never surrender. Nor will my pride tolerate any indignity. So why did You give me ambition and pride?!"

At the mention of the crown and the queen, Hamlet felt his anger rise. He lifted the dagger and was about to plunge it into the king's back when it occurred to him that if his uncle died saying his prayers, there was a chance he would go to heaven. Wouldn't that be doing him a favor? It would, thought Hamlet, and so I'll wait. I will wait for a time when he's unprepared. That way he will go to the fires when he dies, the fires where he sent my father.

He tucked the dagger back into his jacket and slipped out of the room.

"Help, angels!" Hamlet heard Claudius beg as he left. "Bow, stubborn knees! Then all may be well." He laughed at himself. "But it won't be well. My words fly up, but my thoughts remain below. Words without thoughts never to heaven go."

Chapter Eleven

"When he comes, tell him that his antics have angered everyone in the castle." Polonius shook his finger at Gertrude as if he were speaking to his daughter. "Tell him that you are more angry than anyone. His love for you is still clear in his head, and so your charge should cause him some displeasure. Hopefully, it will cut to his very heart, and then we'll have him where we want him." His old eyes sparkled with a cruel glee. "And remember, I'll be hiding here, so do not fear for your person, my lady. Provoke him, trouble him, be hard with him, be . . ."

"I know how to speak to Hamlet," Gertrude said. Her sense of dignity was strong enough to endure just about anything, but Polonius was pushing it. The truth was that she was as upset with Hamlet as anyone in the castle. More than anything else, she wanted Hamlet to be king someday, and his madness was jeopardizing that possibility. If she had to be hard with Hamlet to snap him out of his madness, she would be. If she had to be cruel, she would be. But she did not want Polonius telling her to be hard and cruel. It made her feel as if she were part of the old man's strange game of espionage rather than the Queen of Denmark, the mother of the Prince of Denmark, a woman making sacrifices for the country and the son she loved. "Take your place, and be silent," she said. "I do not fear for my person at the hands of my own son." Footsteps approached the door. "Here he comes. Go."

Polonius slipped behind a thick red curtain that insulated the room against the cold of the stone castle walls.

Hamlet entered his mother's chamber.

"Hamlet," Gertrude said, "your play has much offended your father."

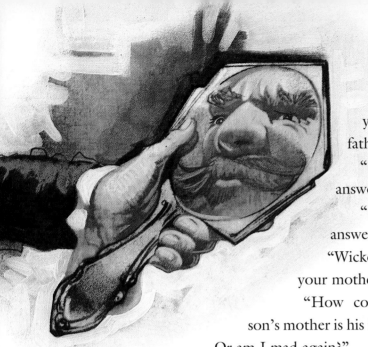

Hamlet sneered. "Mother, your play has much offended my father."

"Come, come," she chided, "you answer with an idle tongue."

"Go, go," said Hamlet, "you answer with a wicked tongue."

"Wicked? Have you forgotten that I am your mother?"

"How could I?" Hamlet answered. "A son's mother is his father's brother's wife, is she not? Or am I mad again?"

"I'll show you mad," said Gertrude, raising her hand to slap some sense into Hamlet.

Hamlet caught Gertrude's hand as she brought it down. He grabbed her other hand too and threw his mother backward into a chair. "It is time you saw what a wicked queen looks like, since you have obviously forgotten." Hamlet took a mirror from his mother's dressing table, but when he turned back to the chair where Gertrude sat, he saw a figure standing behind her.

It was his father's ghost.

"Why, why have you come here, your majesty?" Hamlet asked, his voice trembling.

"This is my bedchamber, Hamlet," Gertrude answered gently, trying to calm her son. "I always come here."

"Not you," Hamlet said. "Him!"

The ghost, not armed this time but in a nightgown, stepped between Hamlet and his mother.

"Him who?"

"Him! Do you see nothing there?"

"Nothing at all, yet all that is there I see."

"Look at him! Don't you see how pale he glares?!"

"Hamlet," said the ghost, his voice seeming to echo from everywhere and nowhere at once. "Do not forget what I told you to do. Revenge is your business, and my brother is your concern. Leave your poor mother alone."

The ghost vanished.

Hamlet dropped the mirror. "Revenge," he said, as if in a trance. He reached for the dagger in his jacket. "Revenge."

Gertrude gasped. Was her son really mad after all? "You're . . . you're not going to murder me, Hamlet?"

"Murder?" came a voice from behind the curtain. "Help! Murder!"

"A rat!" shrieked Hamlet, striking the curtain with his dagger. He felt the blade slice into a body.

"Slain!" coughed someone, falling and ripping the curtain down as he fell. "Slain!"

"What have you done?" Gertrude cried.

His mother's voice felt like cold water on Hamlet's face. "I don't know," he said. When he heard the voice behind the curtain he had acted without thinking, assuming the voice came from Claudius. But, clearheaded now, he knew that his uncle was in his own room praying. So whom had he killed?

Hamlet lifted the curtain and saw Polonius.

"What a bloody deed is this!" said Gertrude.

"Almost as bad as killing a king." He shut
Polonius's eyes. "You wretched, rash,
intruding fool," Hamlet said. "I mis-
took you for your superior."

"Superior?" stammered Gertrude.
"Killing a king? Hamlet, what kind
of talk is this? You're mad. You're
really mad!"

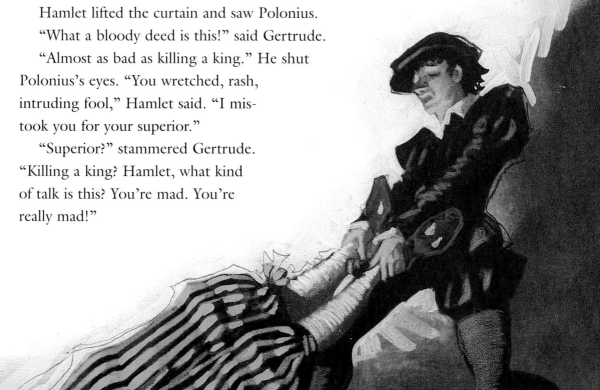

"On the contrary, mother, I have never been more sane." And Hamlet meant it. Watching a man die at his own hand brought home to Hamlet the hard reality of murder and retribution. It was not a matter of ghosts and mad antics and plays. No, it was a matter of life and death, a matter of deciding to take a life and following through on that decision, which also meant accepting the consequences.

"Forgive me, mother," he said. "I must be cruel only to be kind. The king, your husband, murdered my father, your husband. Save your soul and sleep beside him no more. For my part, I shall have an answer for his crime soon enough." He clutched Polonius by the ankles and prepared to drag him out. "As you know I am soon to be escorted to England by Rosencrantz and Guildenstern, whom I trust like adders fanged. Be assured that I will return to see justice done. Relate my words to your husband as your conscience allows."

Gertrude sat in shock. In her darker moments she had wondered whether Claudius did not have something to do with her husband's death, but Claudius had always seemed too faint of heart to plan and commit a murder. Besides, Hamlet's father was dead and gone, regardless of how or by whom, and somebody had to hold Denmark together until Hamlet was mature enough to be the king himself. Someone had to make sure Claudius didn't marry a younger woman who might give birth to a rival prince.

But maybe she had worried too much about Hamlet and not enough about the character of her new husband. Character! She looked at the portraits of her two husbands that hung on the wall. Compared with Hamlet's father, Claudius had no character at all. And she had married him anyway. A woman sometimes has to make sacrifices like that, she told herself, for her son and for her country.

But she had made sacrifices enough. "I won't breathe a word to him, Hamlet." She unfastened her necklace and pulled off the signet ring that belonged to Hamlet's father. "Take this with you to England," she said. "Take it and remember you are your father's son, the Prince of Denmark." She turned away and looked at her tired face in the mirror. "I look forward to your return."

Chapter Twelve

"Go, captain," declared Fortinbras to one of his officers. "Tell the king of Denmark that the armies of Norway intend to march across his lands on our way to Poland." Even though he was no older than Hamlet, the young Norwegian prince bore himself with the regal dignity of a much older man. Sitting tall in the saddle atop a roan stallion, his thick arm laced through a hacked and bloody shield, he looked like the god of war himself. He let the wind dry the sweat from a mane of blond hair before putting his helmet back on.

"If the Dane prefers," he said, "I will tell him face to face." He spurred his horse and rode on, the ox horns of his helmet casting long shadows on the ground before him.

The officer saluted and hurried to carry out his orders.

"Bury him quickly!" hissed Claudius. "I don't want a scandal."

"But my liege," protested the priest. "Polonius was a nobleman. He deserves to be buried with more ceremony."

Claudius looked at the bloodstains soaking

through the sheet that covered Polonius's body, the man Hamlet killed instead of him. He knew the priest was right. Polonius deserved more, but an elaborate funeral would draw too much attention. The people would demand an explanation, and if they learned Hamlet was the murderer, they would assume he had reasons—so much was he loved by all of Denmark. And if the people came looking for reasons, it would just be a matter of time before they discovered the real crime. Claudius's own. And yet, if they buried Polonius quickly and without ceremony, Laertes would suspect foul play and want revenge. Claudius winced at the irony. Of course, a son would want revenge for the murder of his father.

"There is no other way," said Claudius.

The priest understood that there was to be no further argument on the subject. He wheeled the body away to prepare it for burial.

Just then Rosencrantz and Guildenstern rushed in.

"Why haven't you two left for England yet?" demanded Claudius.

"News, my liege," said Guildenstern. "The armies of Norway are marching across Denmark."

"Led by Fortinbras, nephew to the King of Norway," Rosencrantz continued.

"On his way to Poland," Guildenstern added. "Or so the rumor goes."

"Troubles come in bunches," said the king. "But our royal person does not fear the fiery young Fortinbras. We will see to the safety of the kingdom. You two see to the safe transport of Hamlet to England. Immediately. Before he hurts anyone else."

The two young men looked at each other nervously, afraid to leave but afraid not to.

"I take it there's more," said Claudius. "Out with it."

"We received a message," Guildenstern began.

"From Laertes," Rosencrantz continued.

"So he has found out about his father?" said Claudius.

Rosencrantz and Guildenstern gave no answer. They did not have to.

If Laertes, away in France, managed to get wind of the bad news, then surely the rumor was loose among the people of Denmark. Claudius could see it all clearly. Laertes would come marching back home, gathering the angry people around him like a snowball rolling down a hill. They would come to the castle demanding justice.

Then Claudius made a decision. He took a deep breath, pulled out a pen and paper, and wrote:

> *My sovereign brother, the King of England, it is with regret that I tell you that the man before you is a fugitive traitor to be put to death on the authority of the King of Denmark.*

He folded the paper and sealed it with his royal signet.

"Give me the warrant I gave you earlier," he told Rosencrantz and Guildenstern. "Hand this one over instead when you present Hamlet to the King of England. Go now. There is no time to waste."

Chapter Thirteen

Claudius slouched on his throne. Gertrude sat beside him stone still. She watched Ophelia, sitting on the floor at her feet, playing with imaginary flowers.

"There's rosemary, that's for remembrance. Pray you, love, remember." Ophelia pretended to give something to Claudius. "And there is pansies, that's for thoughts." She held out her empty hands to Gertrude.

"I had hoped she would have recovered from the shock," whispered Claudius, "but it has been almost a week now. I fear she has completely lost her mind."

"Her father was her mind," answered Gertrude coldly. "Unless there is a way to bring him back, I fear you are right."

"Humph," snorted Claudius.

"Sweet Ophelia," said the queen gently, "wouldn't you rather lie down?"

"Covered with sweet flowers, she was," Ophelia sang in a faraway voice, "but she went to the grave with no true-love showers." She began to laugh or to cry, it was hard to tell which.

"Take her away," said Claudius, snapping his fingers for a servant. "Try to make her sleep."

As Ophelia was being led away, a commotion was heard outside. Voices shouted, cannons fired, and then came a thumping at The castle gates.

"What noise is this?" asked the queen rising to her feet.

A messenger ran through the doors of the throne room and bolted them behind him. "Save yourselves, my lord and lady!" he yelled. "Laertes has returned and the rabble are calling him 'lord.' They are crying, 'Choose we—Laertes shall be king!'"

Bile rose in Gertrude's throat. Laertes king? All of her plans for Hamlet, all of her sacrifices, were for nothing? "You false Danish dogs," she growled.

The locks on the doors burst open and a sea of people flooded in, led by Laertes.

"Where is this king!" shouted the young man, his voice trembling. He stood with a hand on his rapier.

Gertrude strode courageously out to meet him.

"Let him go, Gertrude!" Claudius, still seated, shouted over the noise of the crowd. "Do not fear for our person. There is a divinity that protects a king from treason. Let him go."

The crowd hushed.

"Now, what is the cause, Laertes," Claudius continued, "of this rebellion?"

"Where is my father!?" demanded Laertes.

"Dead," answered Claudius.

"By whose hand!?" Laertes glared at the king and drew his rapier.

Gertrude took another step towards him.

"Let him ask his fill, our queen," said Claudius raising his hand. "In your concern for your father, Laertes, you prove yourself a good child and a true gentleman, but I am not the murderer."

"But his means of death, his obscure funeral—

no monument over his bones nor formal ceremony—and all at your bidding." Laertes trembled, trying to be bold but too frightened and nervous to be convincing. "Who would not suspect you?"

"Seek what proofs you may, Laertes," said Claudius, "and you will be satisfied that I am blameless. If you discover otherwise, then my crown and my kingdom I give to you." The promise was empty, and Claudius knew it. If Laertes discovered otherwise, Claudius would forfeit his crown and kingdom anyway.

Gertrude was not pleased with that. The kingdom and the crown to Laertes? Since when had Laertes become the Prince of Denmark? Even if her husband were simply trying to buy time by appeasing the overzealous youth, it was far, far too big a promise. She was about to say so when a cry rose from outside the throne room.

The crowd at the door parted to let through a frantic young gentlewoman. Her dress was soaked, and her eyes were streaked with tears.

"What is it, lady?" asked Gertrude.

The woman looked around, not sure whom to address. "Sweet Ophelia," she murmured. "She . . . she is drowned."

Laertes gasped. "My sister?"

Gertrude put her arms around the young woman. "One woe treads upon another's heel," she said. "How drowned?"

"My lady," the woman said, "there is a willow that grows beside the brook whose branches dangle down into the glassy stream. There fantastic garlands did she make of crowflowers, nettles, daisies, and violets." The poor woman tried not to cry as she spoke, but she could not help herself. "There on the hanging willow bough she went to set her wreath of flowers, but the slender limb broke and fell with the lady into the weeping brook. Her clothes spread wide, and mermaid-like a while they bore her up, and in that time she chanted snippets of old songs. But her garments heavy with water . . . pulled her down to a muddy death."

"And now this?" said Laertes, on the brink of tears.

"Take the lady away, Gertrude, and tend to Ophelia," said Claudius. "I will stay with Laertes."

Claudius had to think quickly. Laertes was in shock, but he'd soon snap out of it and want revenge. His only hope lay in the grim letter he had sent to England along with Hamlet. He could still blame it all on the mad prince, but it was crucial that Hamlet never return to Denmark alive to tell the truth.

Chapter Fourteen

"Horatio," whispered a voice hidden in the shadows.

Horatio stopped.

"Horatio," the voice said again.

"Go on ahead, fellow," Horatio said to the gravedigger. "I need to examine these rare flowers. I'll be with you in a moment."

"Suit yourself." The gravedigger thought it odd to study flowers in a cemetery but scholars were always studying strange things. "But let me ask you just one more time. Are you sure we are to give the lady Christian burial? Rumor has it that she took her own life."

"Yes, fellow, Christian burial." Horatio was not one to judge anybody, let alone dead people. "We owe the dead the respect of leaving their final judgment to a higher magistrate than ourselves."

"Well, why do you think I asked you?" joked the gravedigger. "But if it's all right with you it must be all right with God." He shouldered his spade and pickaxe and walked away humming.

"And hurry," Horatio called after him. "They will be here soon with the body."

"She'll wait until the grave is ready," replied the gravedigger. "She's got no other engagements this afternoon."

A saucy fellow, Horatio thought, but he quickly turned his attention toward the voice in the bushes. "Who's there?" he asked.

Hamlet stepped forward. "The Prince of Denmark," he said.

Horatio ran to him. "How can it be, my lord? You are supposed to be in England."

"No, Horatio," Hamlet replied. "I am supposed to be dead."

"I did fear it," said Horatio.

"I myself have stopped fearing it."

Hamlet walked past Horatio and gazed at the graveyard. He seemed to have aged ten years since his departure for England. "I realized Rosencrantz and Guildenstern went with me not as my companions but as my executioners, but on a ship in the middle of the sea one has little hope of escape. I had no choice but to accept that I would not live long enough to see Denmark again, not live long enough to fulfill my promise to my father." He turned to Horatio. "And in that acceptance I changed. You and I have been talking about death and murder as if they were tokens in a game in which honor and manhood were the prize. I know now that we were wrong."

"What happened, my lord?"

"While Rosencrantz and Guildenstern were sleeping, I discovered among their bags a sealed warrant from the king, my uncle," said Hamlet. "It asked the King of England to put me to death upon landing. I was fortunate to have found it, but even more fortunate to have a royal signet of my own." He showed Horatio the ring his mother had given him, the one belonging to his father. "I replaced that warrant with another, one I wrote and sealed myself. It asked the King of England to put Rosencrantz and Guildenstern to death instead. When we disembarked, those two unlucky men presented to the English guard a document that amounted to their own death warrant, signed by my hand." He sighed. "They were arrested on the spot, and I returned at once to Denmark."

"So Rosencrantz and Guildenstern are dead?" asked Horatio.

"As we all must die," Hamlet said, walking slowly among the graves where the undertaker sang a merry song as he dug. "This fellow knows, Horatio. Listen to him sing. He knows all people die, regardless of who they were, when they lived, regardless of whether they were great or ordinary, good or evil. That's why he sings."

The gravedigger let fly a shovel full of dirt and bones, sending a skull rolling toward Hamlet's feet.

"See this skull," Hamlet said. "It could have been the skull of Alexander the Great, and, if it were, it only goes to show that Alexander died, Alexander was buried, and Alexander returned to dust. Just as we all will. There is nothing significant in the death of one man."

"Wrong, wrong, and wrong," said the gravedigger, wiping his nose on his sleeve. "That skull belonged to Yorick. The old king's jester."

"Alas, poor Yorick," said Hamlet, picking up the skull. "I knew him, Horatio, a fellow of infinite jest, of most excellent fancy. He bore me on his back a thousand times. Where are your jests now? Where are your songs?" Hamlet set the skull back down on the ground and brushed the dust from his fingers. "In the end a clown looks no different than a king."

"Does this mean, my lord," Horatio began, knowing he was treading on very delicate ground, "that you now accept the death of your father?"

"Yes and no," Hamlet answered. "My

father was a man and all men die, but all men are not murdered." He folded his arms across his chest and looked up at the sky. "Claudius is a criminal and a traitor, and as a criminal and a traitor it is right that he should die, though whether it is right or wrong he will die at some point. We all must. But," Hamlet said, "if it should fall to me to kill him then I will, but . . . but I do not imagine that my killing him will alter the course of human events."

"And what about the ghost, your father?" Horatio asked.

"Once I thought I needed to kill my uncle to put my father's soul to rest, to keep my mother from sinning, and to save the whole world." He laughed. "Saving souls and rescuing the world! That's a task for a god and not a boy, and only a boy could imagine that such a task fell within his scope." Hamlet stared into his friend's eyes. "If fate decrees that I should be the instrument of my uncle's death, then I shall be. What my uncle's death might mean—I leave for the heavens to figure out."

The sound of priests singing a dirge came from the steep path leading to the graveyard.

"It is the king and queen and . . ." Laertes, Horatio was about to say, but to say so was as much as saying that Ophelia was dead, and he was not sure how Hamlet would react to that. "We should conceal ourselves."

They withdrew back behind the bushes.

The king led the funeral procession, but Laertes followed close behind, his face flushed and his eyes swollen with tears. Gertrude came next with a train of lords and ladies. They gathered around the grave as the pallbearers lowered the casket into the ground.

"Once more!" wept Laertes, "I have to look upon her face once more!" He leapt into the grave.

Claudius tried to stop Laertes, but he could not. Laertes flung open the lid of the coffin and lifted his sister in his arms.

"Ophelia?" Hamlet whispered.

"I . . . I should have told you, my lord," said Horatio.

"Bury us together!" Laertes demanded. "Cover up the living and the dead! O, sweet, sweet Ophelia!"

"Ophelia," Hamlet said again, stepping forward from the bushes. "Ophelia!"

"Hamlet," Claudius said flatly. "You're back."

"My son," gasped Gertrude.

"You!" shouted Laertes. "You are responsible for this!"

"I have no quarrel with you, Laertes," said Hamlet. "But do not prevent me from looking one last time on the woman I loved or from kissing one last time the face I lived to kiss." He too leapt into the grave.

"The devil take your soul!" Laertes spat, dropping the body of his sister and throwing himself on Hamlet.

As the two men struggled, Horatio rushed forward from the bushes and tried to part them before they hurt each other. He managed to restrain Hamlet and lift him out of the grave, as the attendants wrestled Laertes to the ground.

"Peace!" ordered Claudius. "Peace in this churchyard! Let us conclude this solemn ceremony in peace. We will resolve this argument later."

But Gertrude was already restoring peace in her own way.

"Sweets to the sweet," she said, dropping a lily into the grave where Ophelia lay. "I hoped you would have been my Hamlet's wife. I thought I would have covered your bridal bed with flowers, sweet maid, not your grave. Farewell."

All eyes watched the white petals fluttering down into the pit. The undertaker closed the lid of the coffin and everyone watched silently as he filled in the grave.

Chapter Fifteen

The shock Claudius felt upon seeing Hamlet reappear in the cemetery was nothing compared to the terror that set in back at the castle. Hamlet knew his dark secret—and he was alive. Any day, any minute, any second, Hamlet could let the whole world know. What was worse, Hamlet no longer seemed mad. Every day, he carried himself more and more like the true Prince of Denmark,

which meant people would listen to him. What was worse still, Hamlet's transformation made locking him up impossible—let alone killing him. But Claudius was not about to admit failure so soon.

Laertes was still blind with rage and bent on revenge. Laertes was also an expert swordsman. If a confrontation arose between the two young men, Hamlet would surely get the worst of it. Claudius had tried to provoke that confrontation unsuccessfully. He prompted Laertes repeatedly to challenge Hamlet to a duel, but Hamlet answered all of Laertes' requests with heartfelt apologies and entreaties of friendship.

But Claudius had one idea left.

"Laertes," Claudius said, closing the door of the throne room behind him. "I have issued a challenge on your behalf to Hamlet, one that even his mother would not urge him to refuse."

Laertes listened.

"A fencing match," Claudius explained. "Not for blood but for honor. I told Hamlet you didn't think he could hit you twice in ten passes—I told him I bet a jewel he could hit you thrice. He accepted the challenge."

"My liege," objected Laertes, "how will this satisfy my anger?"

Claudius withdrew from his pocket a small envelope filled with a fine white powder. "One drop of this poison will kill five men," Claudius explained, pouring the powder into a cup. "Give me your rapier."

Laertes rarely questioned anything—certainly not his elders and never the king. Yet as he watched Claudius remove the cork tip from the rapier, he began to wonder why the king would want to kill his own nephew. "My liege . . ."

Claudius knew what Laertes was going to ask. "Let us just say that the death of a father should not go unavenged." Claudius dipped the rapier in the cup of poison. "Does this reason satisfy you?"

"Perfectly, my liege," answered Laertes. Tricking someone did not seem exactly honorable to Laertes, especially when the trick would cost that person his life. But if the king said it was all right, Laertes thought, it must be all right.

"Good," said Claudius, striking the air with the rapier before handing it back to Laertes. "I'll keep the poisoned cup close at hand. If you should fail, I will simply offer him a drink."

Hamlet was walking with Horatio in the atrium when Osric rushed in, making a great show of courtesy. "Most excellent, most sovereign, and most gentle sire." He doffed his cap and bent low on one knee. "Laertes is prepared. The most excellent, most sovereign, and most gentle majesty of Denmark waits with him in his throne room, the queen, your mother, by his side."

Hamlet could not help but chuckle at the ridiculous fop. "I thought you said I was the most excellent, most sovereign, and most . . . what else did he say, Horatio?"

"Most gentle, my lord," said Horatio.

"Right," said Hamlet. "All that. How can I and my uncle both be the most," Hamlet shrugged sarcastically, "whatever you said?"

Osric did not know how to respond. "Why, his majesty excels your lordship in years, but . . . but your lordship excels him in promise." Osric bowed again.

"So, if I understand you, you think I am a better man than my uncle, but since he is old, he gets to be the king anyway?" Hamlet asked. "Is that right?"

"I'll go tell the king he said that," said Horatio, pretending to leave.

"No!" exclaimed Osric anxiously. "Please. I did not mean . . ."

"Then you meant that my uncle excels me in years and in character?" said Hamlet.

"He must not think you're much of a prince, my lord," added Horatio.

"No . . . no!" Osric's eyes were wide with fear. "I meant only that . . ."

"What do you want, silly man?" demanded Hamlet, becoming very serious.

"The challenge, your lordship." Osric, completely flushed, fanned himself with his hat. "They await you in the throne room."

"I'll be there in a little while," replied Hamlet.

"But, your lordship," Osric continued, "they await you."

"I. Will. Be. There," Hamlet reiterated, "In. A. Little. While. Do you understand?"

"I do, your lordship, but . . ."

"Then be gone," said Hamlet.

Osric bowed fearfully and ran off.

"What challenge is this, my lord?" asked Horatio.

"Laertes has challenged me to a fencing match," Hamlet explained. "Ten passes."

"You'll lose, my lord."

"I do not think so, Horatio." said Hamlet, "They have given me favorable odds. I need only hit Laertes three times to win, but I have also been practicing lately. And if I lose, so be it. Laertes is still very much the little boy. If winning a game will make him feel like a man, then what is that to me?"

"I fear some plot, my lord," said Horatio. "Don't go."

"Your advice is always not to go, Horatio," returned Hamlet. In truth, Hamlet also feared that Laertes' challenge was more than it seemed, and he shared Horatio's desire to avoid potential trouble, to remain aloof from the world and its problems. But avoiding the problems of the world was a luxury Horatio enjoyed. He was not a prince. Hamlet was. "I thank you for your concern, friend, but if it be now, it is not to come; if it be not to come, it will be now." He smiled.

"My lord . . ."

"Your friend, Horatio. Your friend." Hamlet put a hand on Horatio's shoulder. "Let it be."

Chapter Sixteen

As Hamlet walked slowly but confidently toward the throne room where Laertes waited, he tried to focus on the reasons why he was going. If he were walking into a trap, Hamlet would have to kill Laertes or be killed by him. And if he did kill Laertes, he would then turn his blade on Claudius. But then what? Would he just go to his mother and say that everything was all right now? Would it be all right? Could he go to the balcony, holding up his bloody sword before the people of Denmark, and say that he was now the king?

Did he want to be the king?

He found he could not imagine walking out of the throne room again, which made him wonder if his mind knew something that he did not—that he never would walk out of the throne room again.

As he pushed open the door, Hamlet felt as if he had leapt into the sea. Trumpets blasted and people shouted all around him, but he could not make out individual voices. Rather, the whole assembly seemed to speak in one low, unintelligible note that rose and fell with the beating of his heart, like the roar of the ocean in a drowning man's ear. He saw Claudius lift a cup. He saw his mother standing—as she always stood—a figure of compassionate strength at the right hand of the king. He saw Horatio watching in the recesses. And he saw Laertes—making deft passes in the air with his shimmering rapier.

"Set the cups upon that table," the king called out. "If Hamlet gives the first or second hit, or if he repay Laertes a third time thereafter, let all the battlements fire their ordnance. The king shall drink to Hamlet's better breath. Give me the cups." He raised one of three full goblets from the table. "Let the kettle drum to the trumpet speak, the trumpet to the cannoneer without, the cannons to the heavens, the heaven to earth. Now the king drinks to Hamlet!"

Hamlet ignored him and turned instead to his rival. "The boy who killed your father was mad, Laertes," he said. "Take this hand from the man who used to be that boy and forgive them both."

"I am satisfied in nature," Laertes replied taking Hamlet's hand. "But for honor I must not accept your apology. All of the older gentlemen I spoke with agree that it looks bad to forgive when one's honor has been challenged."

"I understand," Hamlet said. Poor Laertes, he thought. Where will you be when the elders are gone and you are left to make up your own mind?

"Come, begin!" ordered the king.

The drums rolled. The two young men saluted each other and went on guard. Laertes made a quick lunge at Hamlet, but Hamlet blocked the strike with the base of his rapier. Then the blades clacked together at a furious pace. Hamlet dove, Laertes whirled, and the rapiers rang like bells. Laertes faked left to go right, but Hamlet was not fooled. He jabbed the cork tip of his sword into Laertes' chest.

"One," said Hamlet.

"No," said Laertes, pushing the blade away.

"Judges?" said Hamlet.

"A hit, a very palpable hit!" squealed Osric.

"A hit!" bellowed the king. "Let us drink to it!"

The cupbearer lifted the king's goblet from the table.

"And one for me, too," said Gertrude.

Claudius went pale as the queen took the poisoned cup in her hands. "Gertrude, do not drink," he said.

"Pardon me, but I will," Gertrude replied, not sure why her husband was so worried about one little drink. "Won't you have some too, my son?"

"I dare not drink yet, madam," Hamlet said, catching his breath.

"Very well," Gertrude smiled. "But I drink to you." She put her lips to the cup and sipped.

Claudius could not move. She drank.

Too late, Claudius said to himself. It is too late.

"On your guard," said Laertes, stung by having lost a point to Hamlet.

Hamlet raised his rapier and the two clashed again. The blades flashed in the air like lightning. Each time Laertes jabbed, Hamlet blocked; each time Hamlet slashed, Laertes ducked. At last Hamlet took a wrong step and found himself off balance—and he saw Laertes poised to strike.

It was not until the blade cut into his arm that Hamlet realized Laertes had no cork tip on his rapier.

"What villainy is this?" demanded Hamlet. "You who spoke of honor?"

Laertes did not give Hamlet time to say more. He rushed him, pressing him back with a flurry of violent blows.

Hamlet saw the blind fury in Laertes' eyes, and he knew that if he could stay calm he would have a chance to counterstrike.

And he did. Laertes raised his rapier too high, and Hamlet closed in, grabbing Laertes' arm before he had time to bring the weapon down. Hamlet jabbed Laertes in the ribs and twisted his wrist, forcing him to drop his rapier.

Hamlet picked it up and gave his own to Laertes. "Now, let us try that pass again. But this time I'll use your weapon!"

A look of horror came over Laertes' face. He raised Hamlet's rapier to block the blows. Each time the tip of the blade came closer, he saw his own death inscribed upon it, and, distracted, he let his guard down.

Hamlet stuck him between the ribs.

Laertes watched the blood trickle out of the small wound. "Hamlet . . ."

"Ahhhh!" It was Gertrude. She stood once, pointed to the table, and fell.

"She swoons to see them bleed," said Claudius frantically.

"No," coughed Gertrude. "The drink . . . the drink. O, my dear Hamlet! I am poisoned."

Her eyes closed forever.

"Treachery!" Hamlet hissed. "Let the doors be locked. How far does this villainy go?" he said to Laertes.

"No further," Laertes said, tears flowing down his cheeks. "The blade was poisoned, too. There is not a half an hour's life left between us. Exchange forgiveness with me, noble Hamlet. Forgive me."

"I do," said Hamlet. He felt a tremor shake Laertes' body as they embraced. Laertes gasped once and died.

As Hamlet watched Laertes fall beside his mother, he was for an instant gripped with rage. His uncle was to blame for so much death! He wanted to strike off his head—no, he wanted to stab him a thousand times and make him die a slow and agonizing death. No, there had to be something worse. He spun around, rapier in hand, but when he saw his uncle's drooping eyes and drooping shoulders he was moved by pity.

Claudius was a fool, thought Hamlet. Too much ambition and pride to accept the life he was offered by fate, but not enough talent and strength to be anything more.

"Defend me, friends," pleaded Claudius as he saw Hamlet studying him, a rapier at the ready.

"Defend you?" Hamlet asked in disgust. A man of any honor would have dropped to a knee and begged forgiveness for all of his crimes, the ghastly evidence of which lay all around. But his uncle cried out for help—as if he still hoped to salvage something for himself. Such a coward and such a fool, thought Hamlet. And then, in one quick, clean motion, he plunged the blade cleanly into the king's heart.

Claudius died instantly.

Horatio rushed forward. "Quickly, my lord . . ."

"There is no time, Horatio," Hamlet said. Darkness was beginning to creep in on the corners of his vision. "Make a good report of me."

Upon seeing his friend about to die, Horatio was moved by strong emotions, the likes of which he had never felt before. What would it be like in Denmark without the royal family, without his friend? Life would be impossible. He reached for the poisoned cup that still sat on the arm of the queen's throne. "Here's some poison left!" He lifted the cup to his mouth.

With the strength he had remaining, Hamlet swatted the cup from Horatio's hands and fell to the floor.

From outside the castle walls came a volley of cannon fire.

"What warlike noise is this?" asked Hamlet.

Osric ran to the window. "The young Fortinbras!" he cried, watching the banners of Norway flapping in the wind.

Hamlet sighed. "The people will cry out for Fortinbras, and he will be a good king. Give young Fortinbras my dying voice, Horatio. The rest is silence."

Hamlet said no more.

"Good night, sweet prince," said Horatio, closing his friend's eyes.

The doors to the throne room swung open, and Fortinbras strode in, his cape flowing behind him like waves.

"O, proud death," said the Norwegian, surveying the scene. "How many princes have you felled with one shot? Let us haste to hear how this came to pass."

Horatio came forward. "Of that I shall have cause to speak," he said. "But let us first lay these unfortunate souls to rest."

Fortinbras nodded agreement from beneath his horned helmet. "Let four captains bear Hamlet like a soldier to the throne, for he was likely, had he lived, to have proved most royal. And for his passage the soldier's music and the rites of war speak loudly for him. Take up the bodies. Such a sight as this becomes the battlefield, but here shows much amiss. Go," he ordered, "bid the soldiers shoot."

As the servants bore the bodies from the great hall and snuffed out the torches, the low rumble of cannon fire began to echo across the sea.

HAMLET

Because Shakespeare's time was very different from our own, many things that happen in the plays he wrote seem confusing. Knowing what life was like back then helps clear up some of this confusion. Here are the answers to questions *Hamlet* often raises. If you have questions of your own, write me in care of the publisher, and I will try to answer them.

Do the names of the characters mean anything?
Yes and no. Shakespeare borrows many of the names from the books he read, although the more you get to know Shakespeare the more you will want to study the possible reasons for his borrowing one name over another. Fortinbras seems to be a name of Shakespeare's own invention, and it means "strong in arm" in French, a fitting description of the warrior prince of Norway. It is worth knowing that Shakespeare had a son named Hamnet who died not long before Shakespeare started working on *Hamlet*.

What is an arras?
An arras is a beautifully woven cloth named after a town in France then famous for manufacturing them. In medieval times, people who could afford arrases hung them like curtains away from the walls, especially in their bedrooms, in order to make the room smaller and better insulated and thus easier to keep warm. This is why Polonius has enough room to hide behind the arras.

Why does Laertes want to go back to France? Why does Hamlet have to leave Denmark in order to go to school?

Denmark was thought of as a backwater country in Shakespeare's time—but so was England. The wealthiest and most powerful kingdoms in Europe at the time were probably Spain and Turkey, and the great centers of art and learning were in northern Italy. In the Middle Ages, when *Hamlet* is supposed to have taken place, France was the cultural center of the Western world.

Why doesn't Polonius want Ophelia to fall in love with Hamlet?

People watching the play in 1600 would have known that princes and princesses marry for political alliances, not for love. In a way, Polonius is protecting his daughter from disappointment. A marriage with Ophelia would hardly help Denmark defend itself against its powerful enemies (like Norway), and so it would have been bad politically. Also, the class system under which people lived in Shakespeare's time dictated whom a person could marry. Although Ophelia is the daughter of a "gentleman," a person of high social rank, she is still too lowly to marry a prince, although it is interesting that Gertrude does not seem to think so.

Why isn't Hamlet sure if he should trust the ghost?

There were many beliefs about ghosts in Shakespeare's time. According to the Protestant church, which was the official church in England then, there were no ghosts, only devils taking the form of loved ones in order to trick people into sin. However, many people in England still held onto the beliefs of the Roman Catholic church (outlawed about twenty years before Shakespeare was born), in which ghosts were thought to be the souls of people trapped in Purgatory, who were bringing important messages from the next world. Either way, people were far more superstitious then, and ghost sightings were often made the subject of serious investigation.

Why does Claudius refer to himself as "our royal person"?

Kings and queens thought of themselves as having "two bodies," their physical body and their kingdom. For the same reason, kings would often refer to themselves by the name of their kingdom. When Claudius writes, "My brother England," he means the king.

Is the King of England Claudius' brother?

No. Kings and queens used to refer to one another as brothers and sisters, even though they were not really related. It was a way of acknowledging that they were members of a small and elite group of very special people.

Why is the gravedigger worried about burying Ophelia in a cemetery?

Cemeteries were—and still are—considered sacred ground. In Shakespeare's time, anyone who took his or her own life was not allowed "Christian burial" in a cemetery. It was a way of recognizing that the soul of the person would never be at rest. Sometimes those unfortunate people who did take their own lives were buried at a crossroads, which, at the time, people thought would keep the restless souls from wandering.

If Hamlet is the prince, why didn't he become the king when his father died?

There is no easy answer to this question. It was not uncommon for a "regent" to act as head of state when a child inherited the throne, but Hamlet is certainly not a child. It helps to know that the play was written when Queen Elizabeth was very old and heading toward death without having ever married or had children. For this reason, everyone in England was extremely concerned about the "succession," which means the passing along of the kingdom from one rightful monarch to the next. Claudius is obviously not the rightful monarch, and so the play shows what can happen when the wrong person takes the throne.

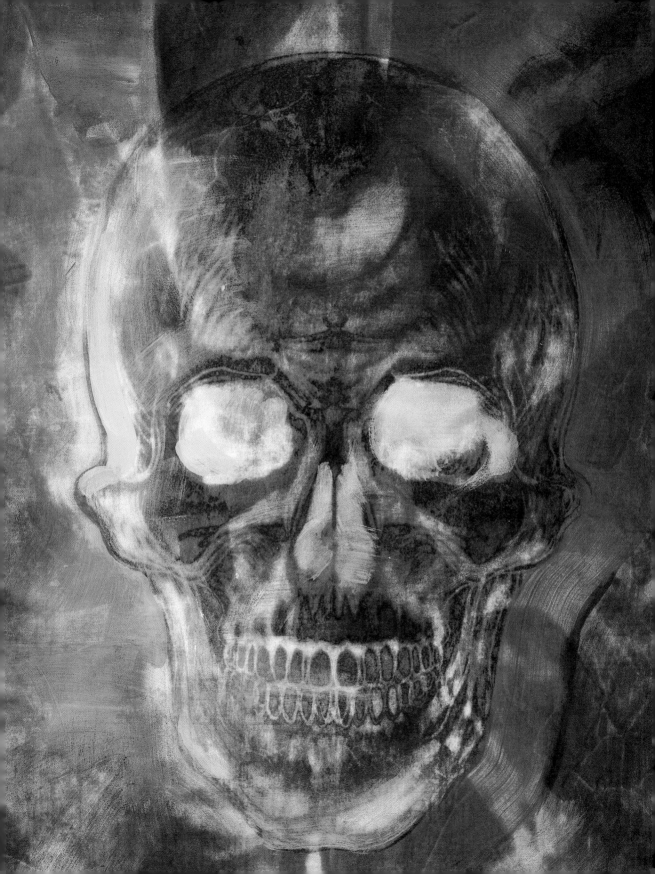

WHO'S WHO IN
HAMLET

BARNARDO: a guard at the palace

CLAUDIUS: King of Denmark and Hamlet's uncle

FRANCISCO: a guard at the palace

FORTINBRAS: nephew of the King of Norway and heir to the throne

GERTRUDE: Queen of Denmark and Hamlet's mother

GHOST: a spirit that seems to be Hamlet's father

GUILDENSTERN: a young gentleman and Hamlet's acquaintance

HAMLET: Prince of Denmark

HORATIO: a scholar and close friend of Hamlet

LAERTES: Polonius's son and Ophelia's brother

OPHELIA: Polonius's daughter

OSRIC: a gentleman at the service of the king

POLONIUS: an advisor to the king and father of Ophelia and Laertes

ROSENCRANTZ: a young gentleman and close friend of Guildenstern

INDEX